BIG, BUSY ADVENTURE BAY

By Cara Stevens
Illustrated by Dave Aikins

Random House 🏠 New York

rhcbooks.com
ISBN 978-0-593-17266-7 (trade)
MANUFACTURED IN CHINA
10 9 8 7 6 5 4 3 2

eagle

periscope

control panel

flower

table

chair

PupPad

rug

INSIDE THE LOOKOUT

It's a busy day in Adventure Bay. Ryder has called the PAW Patrol to the Lookout.

"Good morning, pups! We have a busy day ahead of us," he says. "We have a big event at city hall, a race at the raceway, and a super-fun carnival—plus Luke Stars has asked us to be in his music video!"

The pups are excited to join in the fun. They know that with teamwork, they can help make even the busiest day run smoothly. The PAW Patrol is ready to roll!

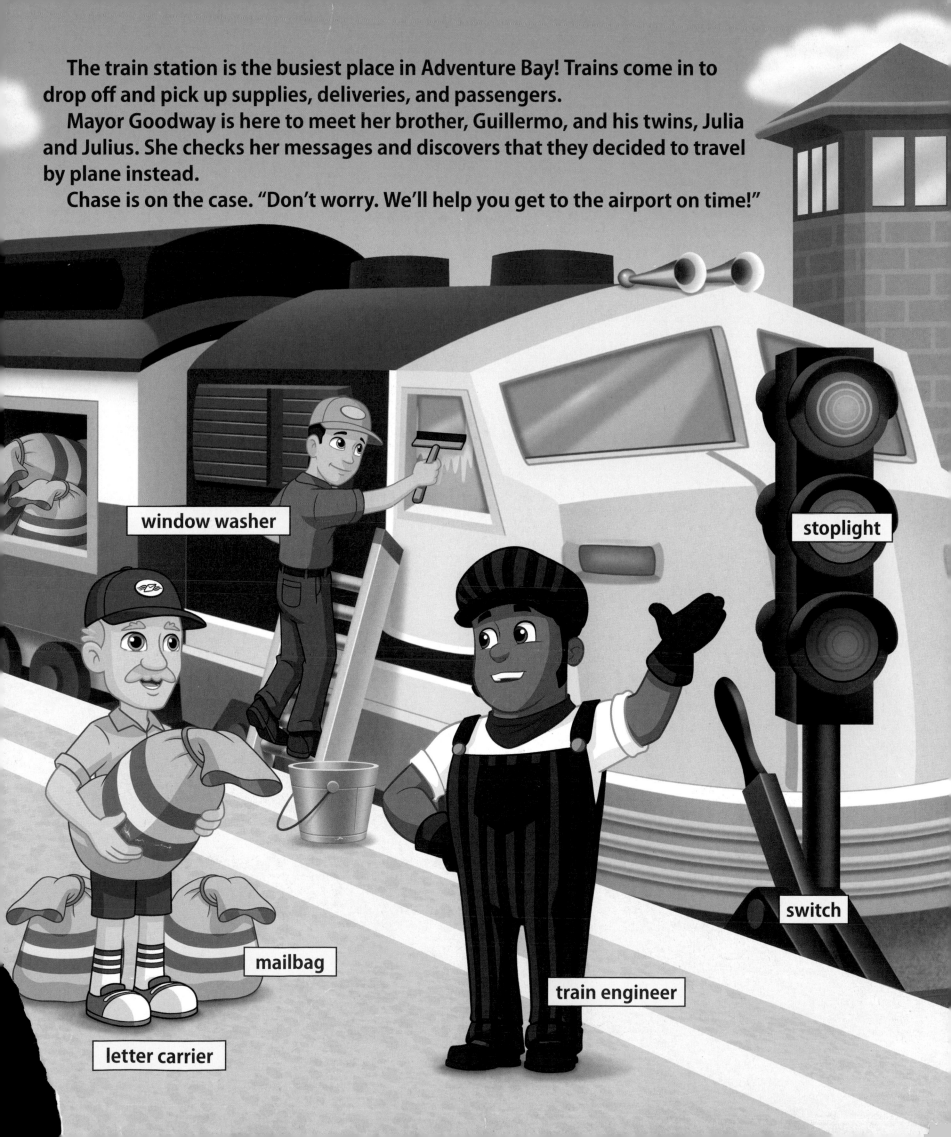

The train station is the busiest place in Adventure Bay! Trains come in to drop off and pick up supplies, deliveries, and passengers.

Mayor Goodway is here to meet her brother, Guillermo, and his twins, Julia and Julius. She checks her messages and discovers that they decided to travel by plane instead.

Chase is on the case. "Don't worry. We'll help you get to the airport on time!"

window washer

stoplight

switch

mailbag

train engineer

letter carrier

THE PAW PATROLLER

Robo Dog has responded to Ryder's call. Mayor Goodway, Ryder, and the pups have all piled into the PAW Patroller. This eighteen-wheeled vehicle lets Ryder and the pups take their rescue skills on the road. It's also the fastest way to get Mayor Goodway to the airport on time! The PAW Patroller has all the team needs, including snacks and rescue vehicles!

fan

comfy cushion

tools

AIRPORT

The Adventure Bay Airport is a very busy place. With so many people coming and going, it's a good thing Chase is here to direct traffic! Mayor Goodway is worried. "It's so busy, I hope I can find my family."

surfboard

flight crew

underwear

suitcase

Oh, no! Someone left the penguins' carrier door unlocked, and now they're causing major mayhem. Ryder thinks fast. "I know something that will get those penguins back in line!"

excited penguin

luggage cart

ice cream bar

golf clubs

backpack

hangar

mail plane

wind sock

fuel truck

airport bus

portable staircase

luggage

Outside the airport, things are even busier. Some planes are landing, and others are roaring into the sky! On the ground, Rocky helps the mechanics check the engines and fill the jets' tanks with fuel. The planes also need to be loaded with luggage, snacks, and packages. Rubble is ready to pull the heavy loads.

Ryder is getting a distress call from Katie.

"Don't worry, Katie," he says. "The PAW Patrol is on a roll!"

control tower

airplane

runway

CONSTRUCTION SITE

Cali has chased a butterfly onto the construction site! Katie calls Ryder to let him know the pups are on the case.

"It's a good thing Katie called," says Ryder. "You should never go onto a construction site alone."

At the site, workers are building a new house. The plumber is laying pipes for water. The bricklayer is building a chimney for a fireplace.

What a busy place. Stay safe, everyone! Don't forget to wear your hard hats.

fish

butterfly

digger

pipe

plumber

FIRE STATION

While the rest of the pack is rescuing Cali, Marshall pays a visit to the fire station. With all the activity going on in Adventure Bay, Marshall wants to be sure the town's rescue teams are prepared in case of an emergency.

hook

helmet

jacket

fire engine

hose

ladder

towel

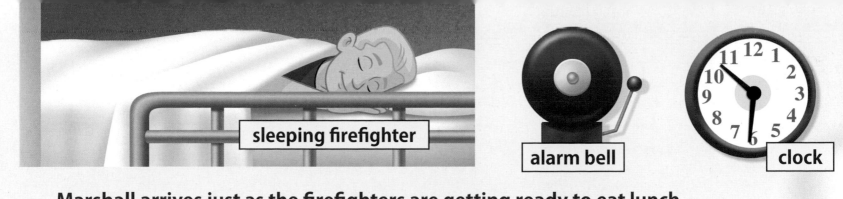

sleeping firefighter

alarm bell

clock

Marshall arrives just as the firefighters are getting ready to eat lunch. "Someone should really be watching the soup," Marshall tells the fire chief. Can you find other things that need attention at the station?

fire pole

smoke

first aid kit

leaky faucet

fire

stove

plates

candle

cup

boot

CITY HALL

tree

lamppost

camera

stroller

scooter

recycling bin

flag

statue

drum

Mayor Goodway and her brother, Guillermo, have arrived at city hall for the dedication of a new statue of their great-great-great-great-grandfather Grover Goodway, Adventure Bay's first mayor. The twins are excited to be part of the celebration, too. But where has Chickaletta flown off to? The mayor is worried it won't be a proper celebration without her.

"Don't worry, Mayor Goodway," says Chase. "Skye will find her in no time!"

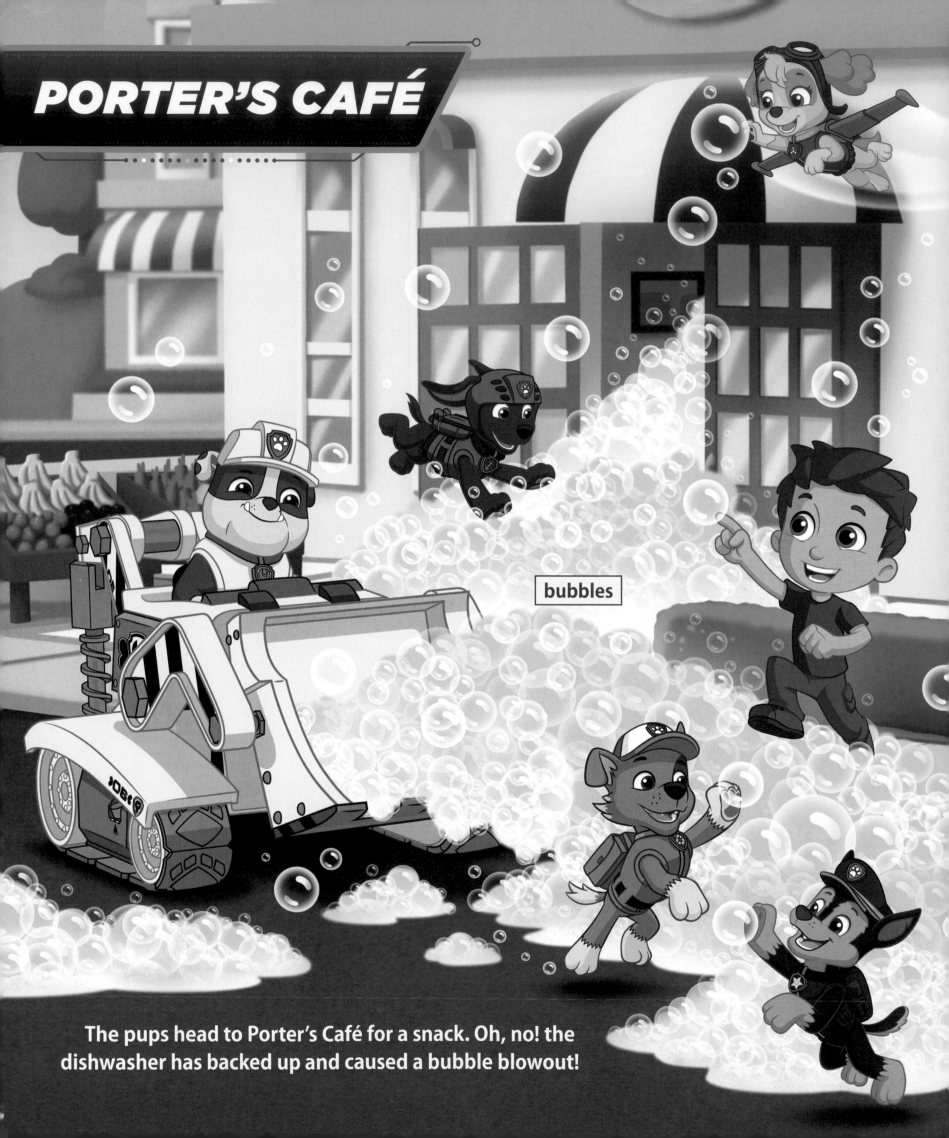

PORTER'S CAFÉ

bubbles

The pups head to Porter's Café for a snack. Oh, no! the dishwasher has backed up and caused a bubble blowout!

flag

statue

drum

Mayor Goodway and her brother, Guillermo, have arrived at city hall for the dedication of a new statue of their great-great-great-great-grandfather Grover Goodway, Adventure Bay's first mayor. The twins are excited to be part of the celebration, too. But where has Chickaletta flown off to? The mayor is worried it won't be a proper celebration without her.

"Don't worry, Mayor Goodway," says Chase. "Skye will find her in no time!"

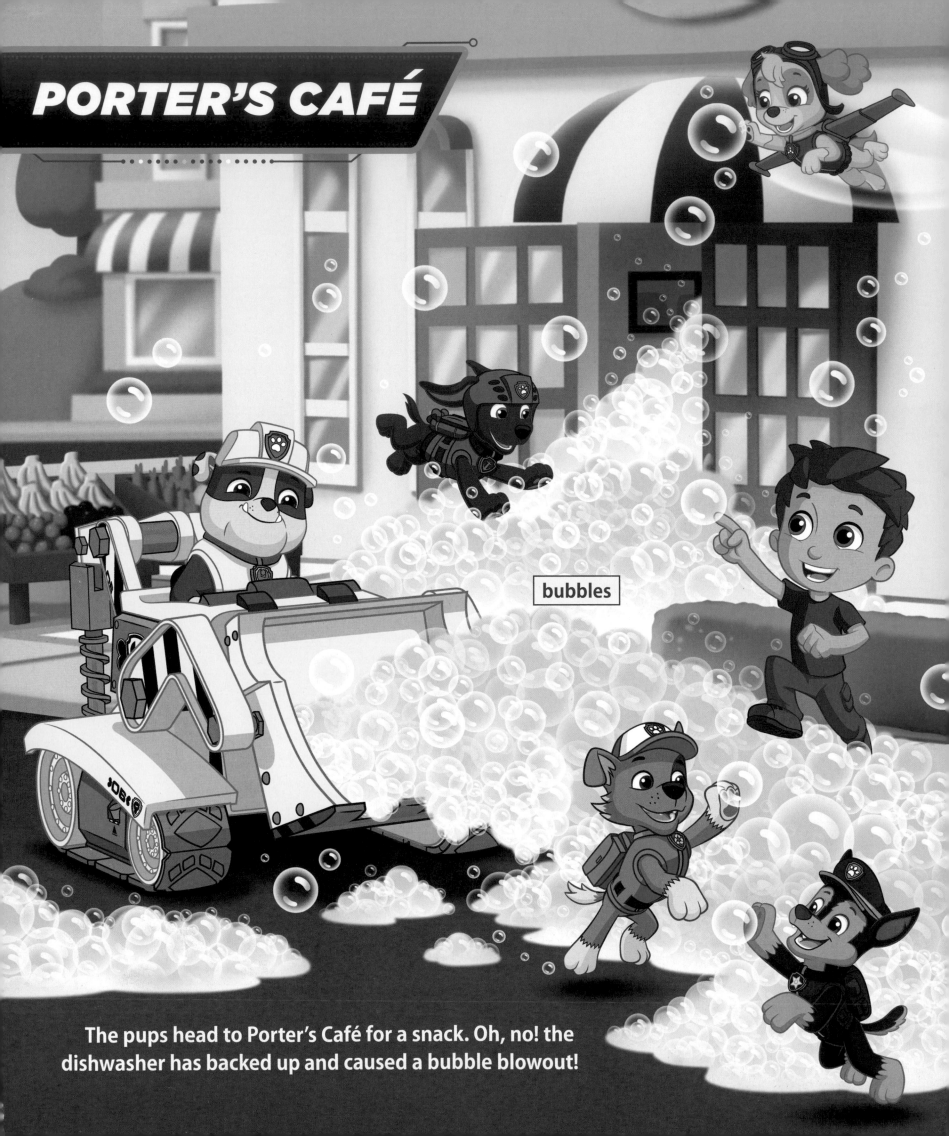

PORTER'S CAFÉ

bubbles

The pups head to Porter's Café for a snack. Oh, no! the
dishwasher has backed up and caused a bubble blowout!

FRUITS & VEGE[TABLES]

umbrella

awning

pup bowls

bananas

watermelons

scale

fruit stand

corn

crate

trash can

spilled milk

The PAW Patrol races to the rescue. Zuma dives in to turn off the water while the rest of the pups help Alex pop the bubbles. Cleaning up is fun when you do it with friends!

Farmer Yumi calls Ryder to help with the apple harvest.

"There's a storm on the way, and we need to collect the apples before they're ruined," says Farmer Yumi.

The pups arrive as quickly as they can.

"Rubble on the double!" says Rubble.

Rocky finds a rain gutter that's perfect for the harvest. "Don't lose it—reuse it!" he says with a smile.

Marshall sends the apples down Rocky's fruit chute while Rubble collects them.

apples

horse

rain gutter

mailbox

basket

When they're all done, Farmer Yumi gives each pup an apple to thank them for their help. What a sweet reward!

FARMER YUMI'S FARM

beaver

goat

pig

rake

Bettina the cow

hay bale

sheep

pumpkins

chickens

rabbit

carrot patch

SCHOOL

Alex's teacher has invited Ryder and the pups for a class visit. Marshall talks about fire safety. Chase reminds the class to buckle up in the car, and wear a helmet and safety gear when riding a bicycle. Rocky shows everyone how to recycle paper and plastic and how to compost fruit and vegetable waste.

teacher

paintbrushes

easel

paint

desk

students

map

fire alarm

calendar

HELMET

fire extinguisher

chalk board

plastic bottle

eggshells

scrap paper

banana peel

scissors

paper

notebook

pencil

security camera

Chickaletta's feather

portrait

guard

ship in a bottle

bench

MUSEUM

The class is going on a field trip. Ryder and the pups are invited to come along!
A museum guide tells the visitors stories about all the items in the museum's collection.

painting

airplane

guide

dinosaur fossil

sculpture

"There are so many interesting things to see here," says Skye.
Rubble is especially interested in the extra-large dinosaur skeleton.
"That fossil is millions of years old, Rubble," says Ryder. "You won't
find any meat on those bones!"

LIBRARY

window

Oh, no! Ms. Marjorie has brought her pet raccoon, Maynard, to the library. Now Maynard is stuck on a bookcase, and it's taking a pack of pups to rescue the reckless raccoon!

"Please rescue him quietly! This is a library!" says Ms. Marjorie.

Marshall isn't watching his step and slips on a book. "I'm okay!" he says, laughing as he tumbles head over heels.

volunteer

boat book

lamp

eyeglasses

bookcases

net

claw

books

ADVENTURE BEACH

pineapple

coconut drink

ukulele

seashell

Mayor Goodway, Katie, and Mr. Porter are having a super-special Hawaiian luau. Ryder asks the PAW Patrol to help, too. They will be lifeguards.

"Lifeguards are in charge of keeping everyone safe on the beach and in the water," Ryder explains.

beach umbrella

beach chair

lifeguard stand

whistle

sandcastle

starfish

crab

"Sea Patrol ready for action, Captain Ryder, sir!"
Chase replies.
Chase patrols the sand while Skye and Rocky
watch the water from the lifeguard chairs.

"A serious storm is simmering from the south, and I have a horrible hole in my hull!" Cap'n Turbot exclaims.

sailboat

patch

towrope

hull

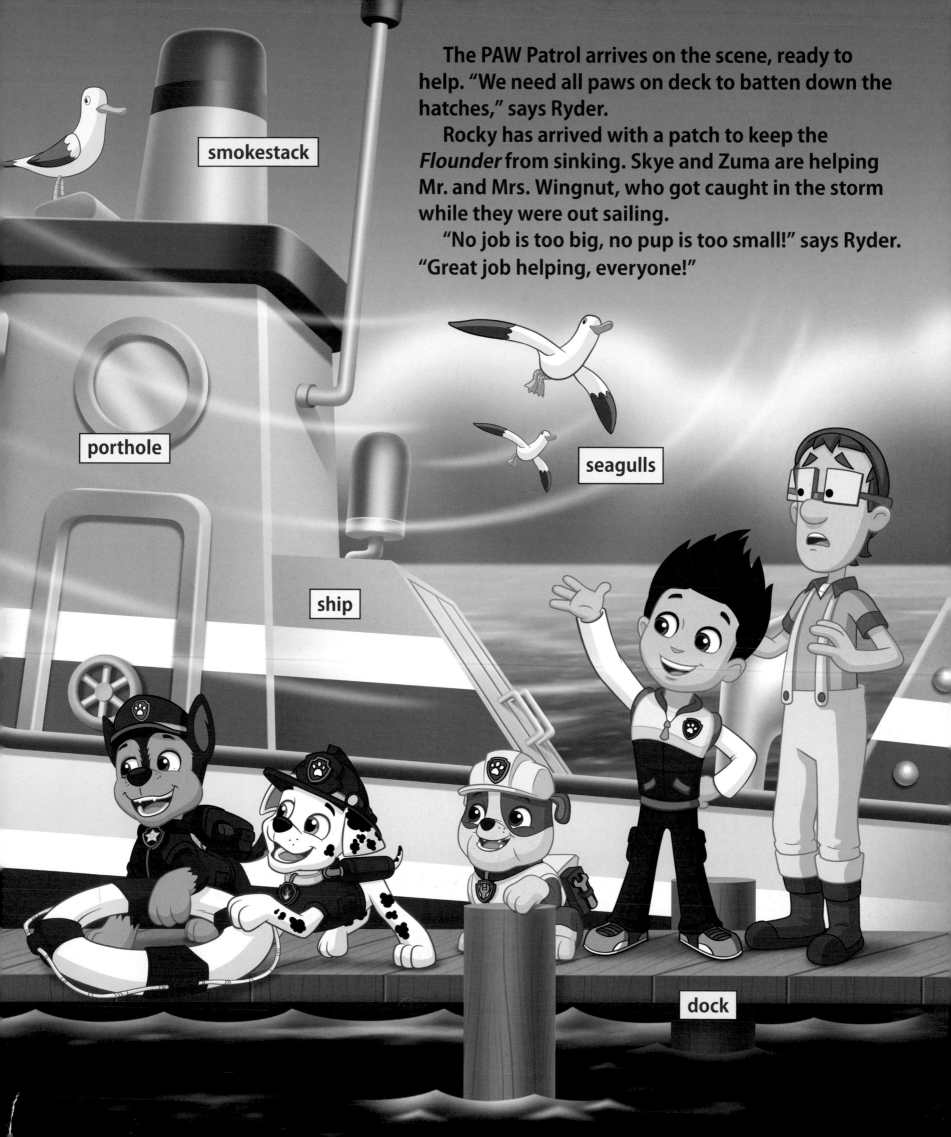

The PAW Patrol arrives on the scene, ready to help. "We need all paws on deck to batten down the hatches," says Ryder.

Rocky has arrived with a patch to keep the *Flounder* from sinking. Skye and Zuma are helping Mr. and Mrs. Wingnut, who got caught in the storm while they were out sailing.

"No job is too big, no pup is too small!" says Ryder. "Great job helping, everyone!"

smokestack

porthole

seagulls

ship

dock

helicopter landing pad

lifeguard

cake

cookies

zip line

deck

basketball hoop

Ping-Pong table

A cruise ship is visiting Adventure Bay for the day. Ryder asks the pups to make sure everything is shipshape after the big storm.

Once Marshall and Rubble see that all is well, they're excited to check out the ship's offerings—especially the dessert table!

"Ready, set, get wet!" Zuma shouts gleefully as he splashes down the waterslide.

"That water is a little too wet for me," Rocky says.

waterslide

mop

bucket

pool

MOVIE SET

Luke Stars is in town to make a music video, and he has invited the PAW Patrol to be in a scene. There are many people on the set. It takes a lot of them to shoot a video!

Marshall is all fired up, but he's also nervous. "Don't worry—you'll be great!" Luke reassures him.

monitor

director chair

microphone

video camera

makeup artist

hairstylist

daredevil

Oh, no! Somehow Ryder's friend Danny ended up in the scene, too, and he's insisting that everyone call him Daring Danny X.

"I hope Danny plays it safe," Skye says, looking worried.

spotlight

autograph books

excited fans

Poor Daring Danny X. His daredevil stunt didn't go very well. Fortunately, the PAW Patrol was there to spring into action with a daring rescue. Marshall took care of Danny until an ambulance arrived to get him to the hospital for X-rays.

nurse

X-ray

cast

crutches

doctor

The hospital is bustling with activity. Everyone there is friendly and helpful. "You'll be all patched up in no time, but be more careful!" the doctor tells Danny. "We'll keep an eye on him, Doctor," Ryder promises.

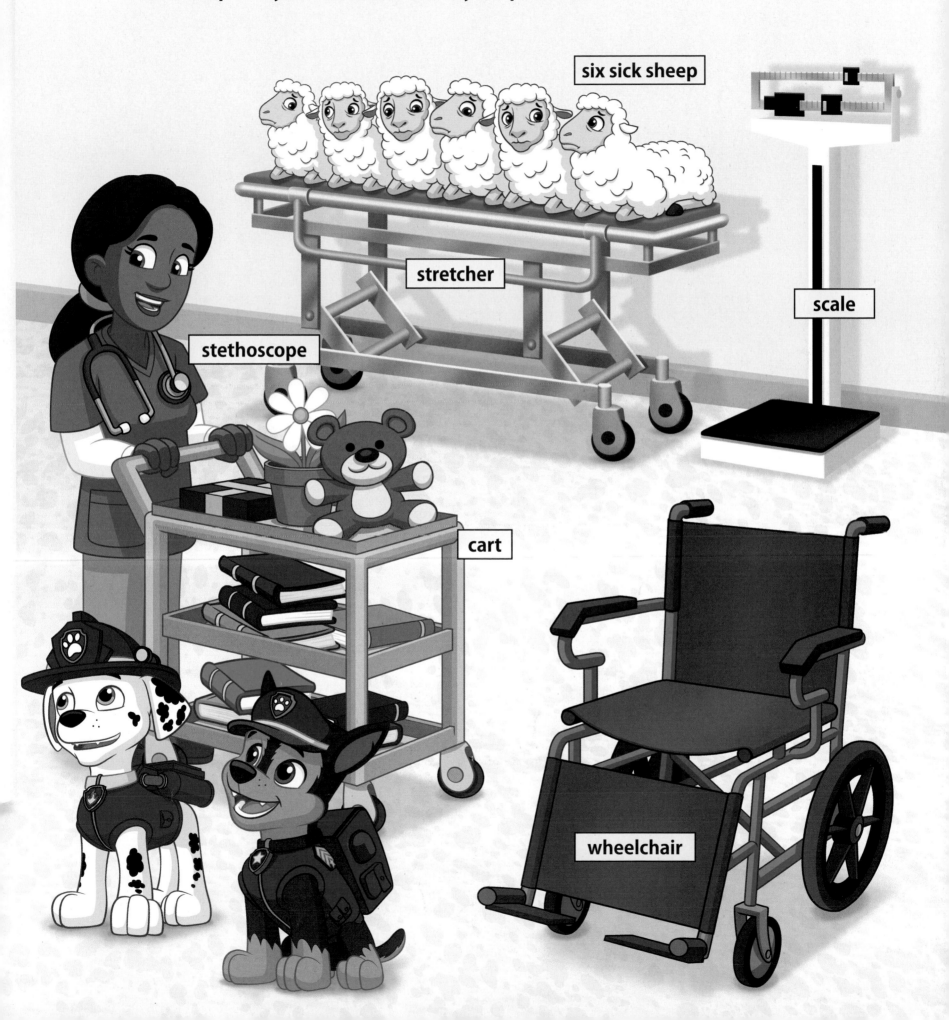

six sick sheep

scale

stretcher

stethoscope

cart

wheelchair

PARK

ball

runner

playground

skateboard

The pups have worked hard all day. Now it's time to play! Rocky is looking for someone to ride on the seesaw with him.

"I'll play with you, Rocky!" Alex shouts happily.

"Alex, *paw*-some job recycling that can!" says Rocky.

Marshall has brought snacks to feed his friend Fuzzy, the baby goose.

Uh-oh! Someone forgot to put their skateboard away. Marshall trips.

"I'm okay!" Marshall says, laughing.

kite

slide

Hula-Hoop

pitcher

pizza

seeds

Ryder and the pups arrive at the recycling plant to drop off some items. "The things you get rid of have to go somewhere," says Rocky. "Some things can be recycled or turned into something new." At the recycling plant, trash is sorted into a bin. Plants, fruits, vegetables, and other green waste gets turned into material called compost that can help new plants grow. And recycled items are sorted so they can be used in new ways. Some of the trash gets taken to the power plant to be burned as fuel. Other things, like books, can be given away instead of thrown away.

"Don't lose it—reuse it!" Rocky says.

flies

chute

dump truck

sorting bins

box

propeller

spare tire

UNDERWATER SYSTEMS

A water pipe has burst! Here comes Rubble, on the double! Rubble digs to find the broken pipe while Rocky searches his recycling truck for a patch to put on the hole.

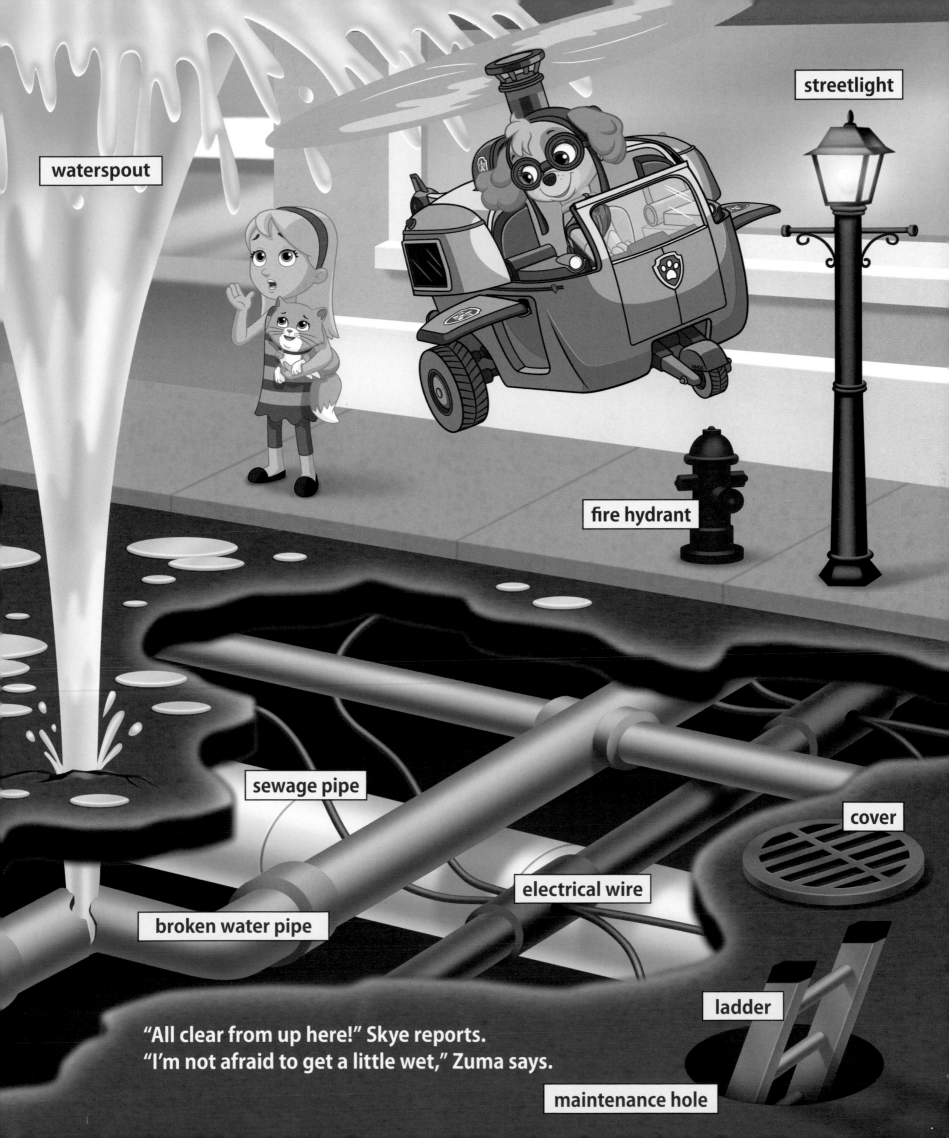

waterspout

streetlight

fire hydrant

sewage pipe

cover

electrical wire

broken water pipe

ladder

"All clear from up here!" Skye reports.
"I'm not afraid to get a little wet," Zuma says.

maintenance hole

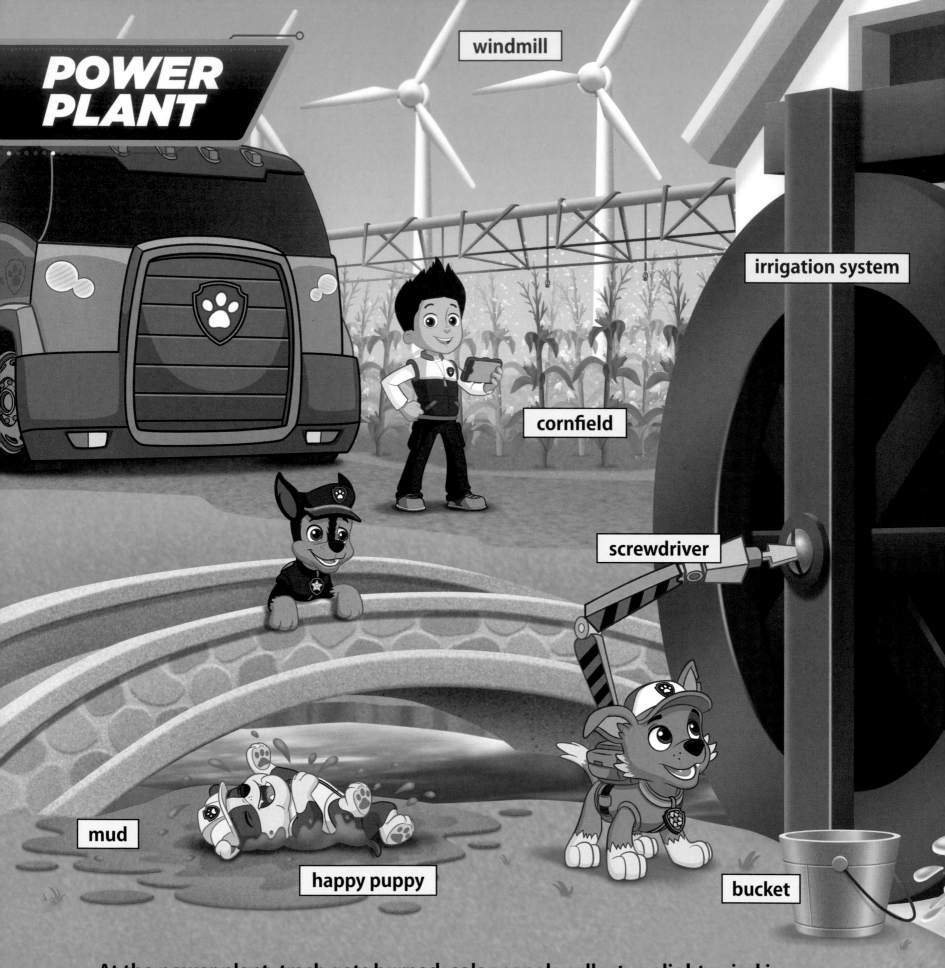

POWER PLANT

windmill

irrigation system

cornfield

screwdriver

mud

happy puppy

bucket

At the power plant, trash gets burned, solar panels collect sunlight, wind is harvested by windmills, and running water powers a generator. They are all sources of energy that keep electricity flowing to the homes and businesses of Adventure Bay. Ryder and the pups are checking in at the power plant to make sure everything is going smoothly.

solar panels

power line

waterwheel

power generator

burning trash

power plant worker

river

Rocky is using his Pup Pack to tighten a screw in the waterwheel.
Zuma makes sure everything is working properly below the surface.
"Ready to dive in!" Zuma announces. *Splash!*

AIR PATROLLER

Ryder and the pups are responding to an urgent call from Jake, up on the mountain. A sudden snowfall has trapped a baby bear on a cliff, and it's up to the PAW Patrol to go to the rescue!

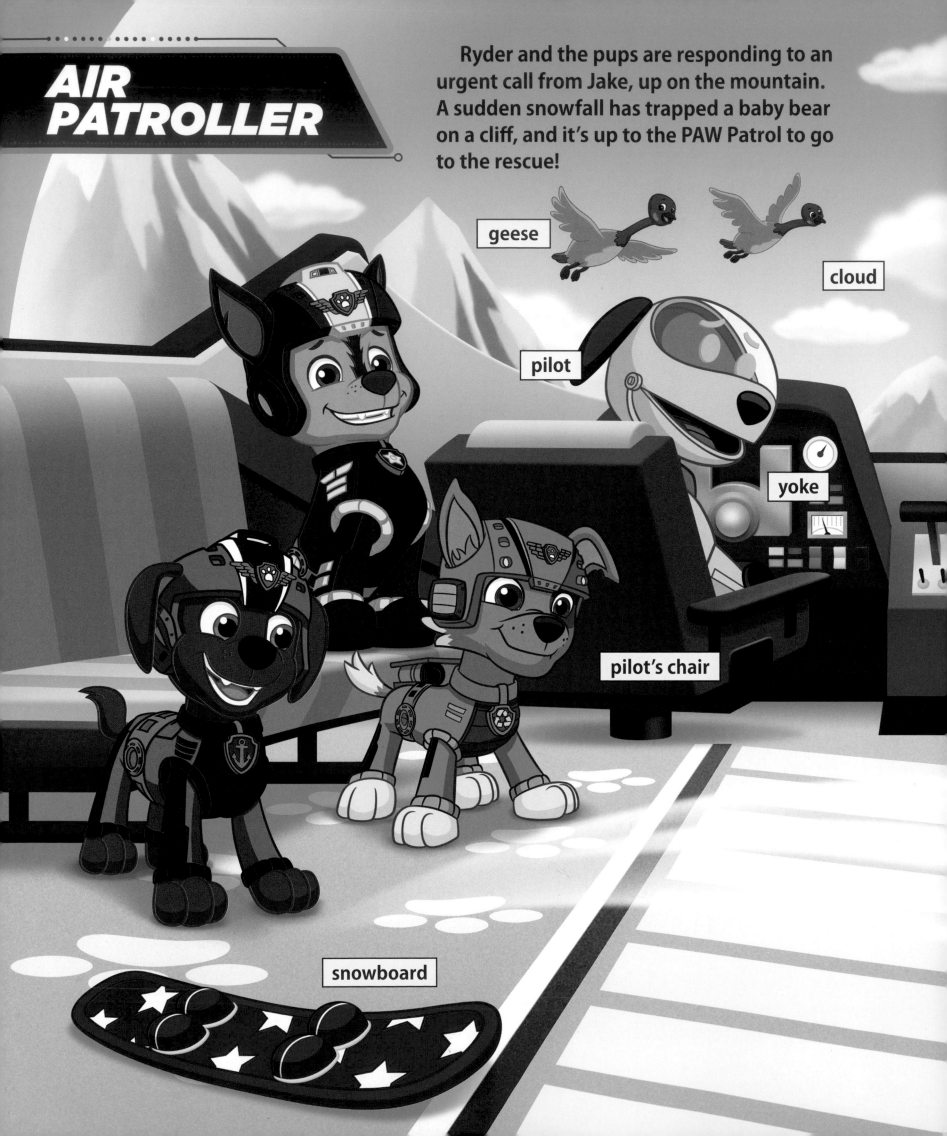

geese

cloud

pilot

yoke

pilot's chair

snowboard

Marshall isn't a fan of flying, but he knows the baby bear needs help, so he rushes in before he can change his mind. "No running in the Air Patroller, Marshall!" Ryder reminds him. It's a good thing there are traffic cones to slow his roll!

peak

mountain

hot-air balloons

copilot

view screen

copilot's chair

traffic cones

JAKE'S MOUNTAIN

Robo Dog sets the Air Patroller down gently in the snow. Everest and Jake are there to meet the PAW Patrol.

"You arrived just in time. The baby bear is on a ledge that's about to break!" Jake says.

Rubble and Everest quickly clear a path with their snowplows.

Air Patroller

snowpeople

lodge

snowballs

ski lift

ski hat

slope

mama bear

baby bear

ledge

pine trees

Skye fits Chase into a harness and lowers him as close to the baby bear as she can.
The rescue mission is a success!
"I love rescues!" Everest says giving Rubble a high paw.

CARNIVAL

At the Adventure Bay Carnival, Cap'n Turbot's big balloon bouncer has burst its bubble! Skye pumps it with air while Marshall waits with a patch to close up the hole.

"I'd sure like to win one of those cute stuffed animals," Skye says.

balloons

bounce house

air pump

face painter

After the carnival, everyone heads to the track.

prizes

popcorn

corn dog

clown

lemonade

target

unicycle

fence

wagon

jumbo screen

trophy

racing helmet

race car

tire iron

starting line

wrench

The Adventure Bay 500 is the biggest race of the year. The fastest racers are gathered at the starting line. The PAW Patrol is on the scene with their Mobile Pit Stop. "The pit-crew pups are here to help!" Ryder announces.

Skye does a safety check to see that everyone is wearing seat belts and helmets. Ryder, Rubble, and Rocky are tightening the bolts on the wheels and tuning up the engines.

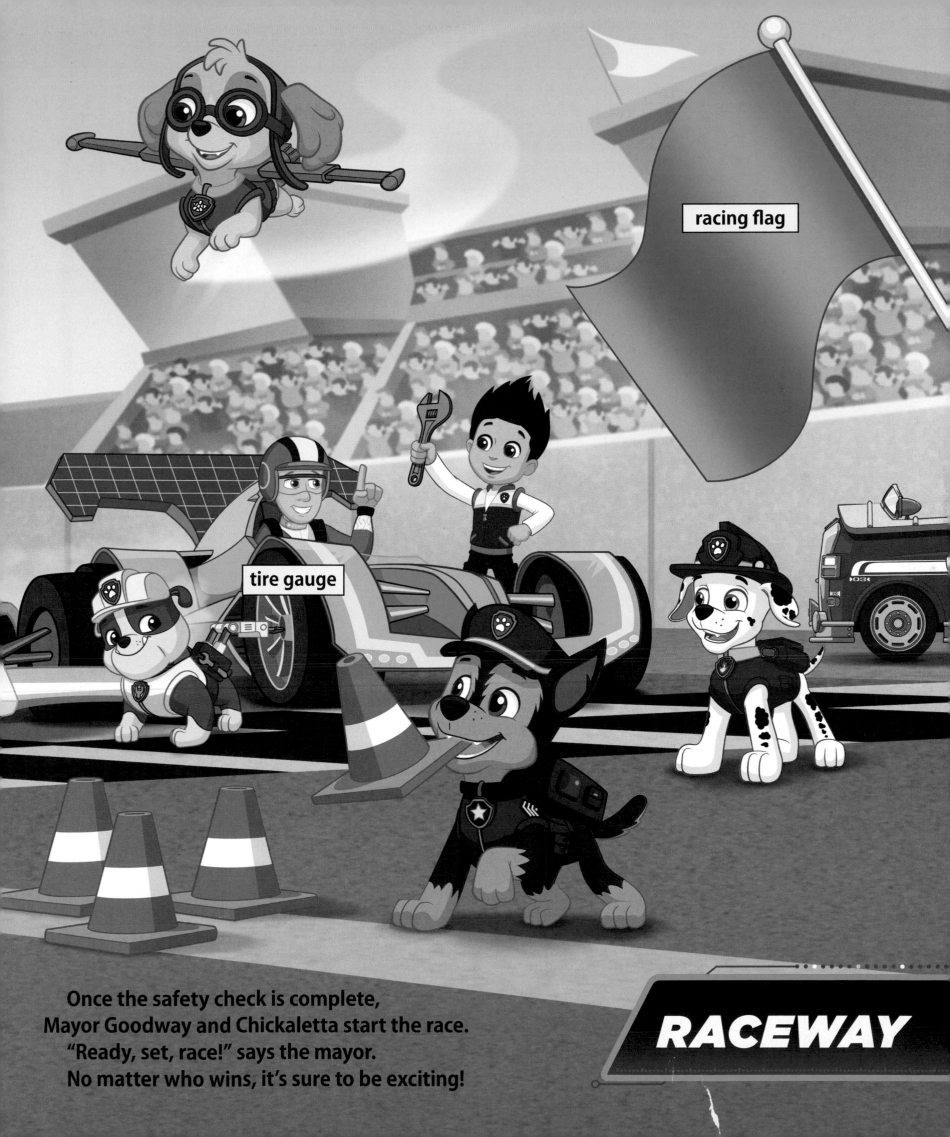

racing flag

tire gauge

RACEWAY

Once the safety check is complete,
Mayor Goodway and Chickaletta start the race.
"Ready, set, race!" says the mayor.
No matter who wins, it's sure to be exciting!

PUP HOUSES

It's nighttime in Adventure Bay. After a long day, the pups are on a roll . . . right into bed! Rocky washes up. Zuma has a bedtime snack.

mirror

toothbrush

toothpaste

blanket

hand towel

bedtime snacks

pajamas

bath toy

towel

soap

bathtub

sponge

Rubble enjoys a bubbly face wash. Skye reads a bedtime story.
Marshall is already fast asleep!
"Ready for bedtime, Ryder, sir," Chase says.
"Good night, pups!" Ryder replies.
No dream is too big, no pup is too small!

night-light

dog bed

nightcap

pillow

teddy bear

bedtime stories

stuffed animals

stars

owls

skunk

firefly

OUTSIDE THE LOOKOUT

Hootie the owl and all his nighttime friends are on patrol, keeping watch over Adventure Bay while everyone sleeps.

When morning comes, Maynard the raccoon, Bayberry the skunk, and the other animals will go to sleep. Ryder and the pups will wake up refreshed and ready to start another busy day in Adventure Bay!

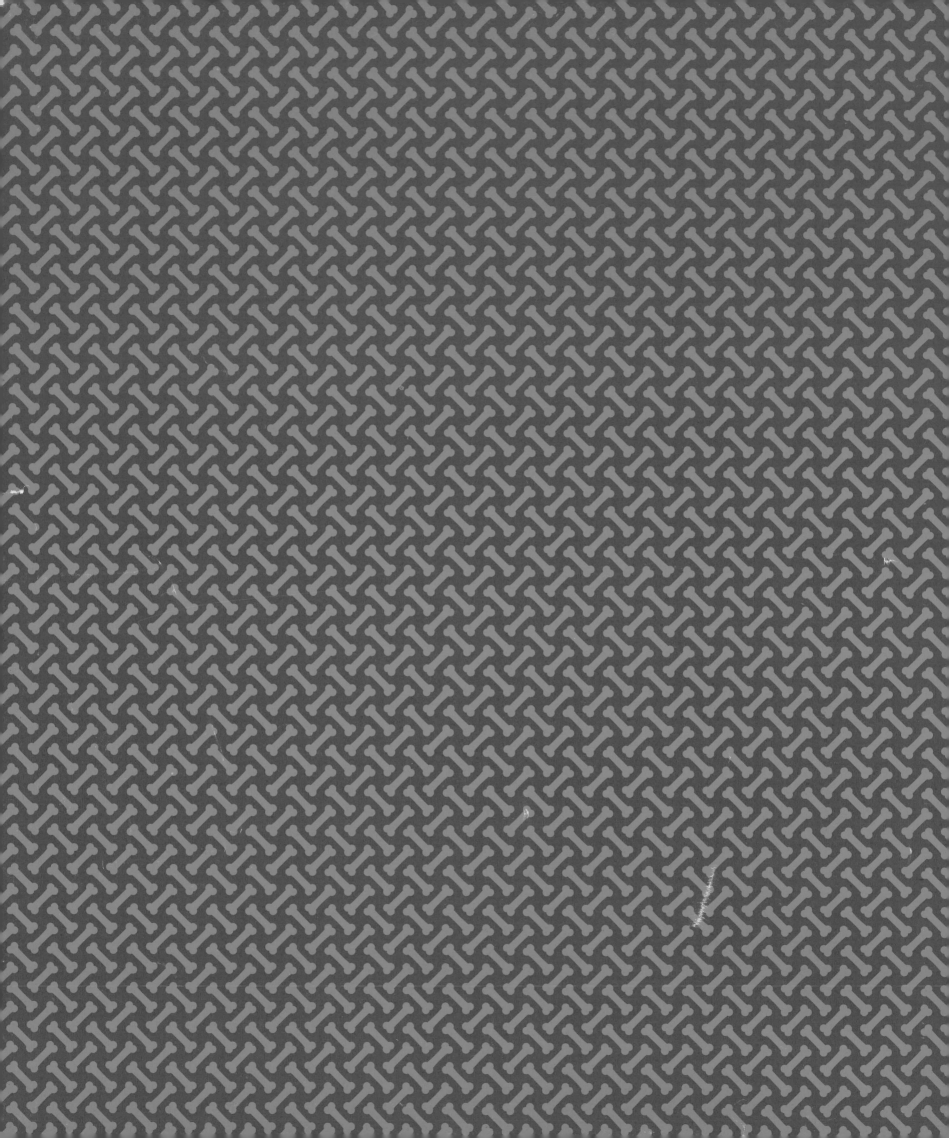